GRIZZLY BEAR
by Berniece Freschet
drawings by Donald Carrick

CHARLES SCRIBNER'S SONS · NEW YORK

In the middle of a shrieking January blizzard, high on a mountain in Montana, Bear Baby was born.

A few minutes later, in the same mountain cave, another cub was born.

The grizzly cubs came into the world with their eyes tightly shut. They had very little hair and no teeth, and they were very small—not even as big as their mother's paw.

Bear Baby whimpered. He was hungry.

The tiny cub pulled himself through his mother's thick coat of fur. He must find food—and quickly. But it was his brother who found the first nipple of milk.

The little newborn cub was very weak. Whimpering, Bear Baby struggled through the long hairs, clinging to the shaggy fur, slowly pushing upward.

Then his mouth closed around a firm, smooth button, and he sucked hungrily.

He made a soft hum of contentment as the rich, warm milk trickled down his throat. When his stomach was stretched tight, Bear Baby slept.

This first fight for life by the newborn cub was a sign of his future—nothing was to come easy for Bear Baby.

Cold, blizzard winds howled outside their cave, but inside, the small cubs were safe and warm, snuggled deep in their mother's shaggy fur.

The bear cubs spent most of their time sleeping, waking only now and then to nurse.

Because of his mother's rich milk, Bear Baby grew rapidly. When he was three weeks old his eyes were still closed, but now he and his brother began to crawl about the cave.

Once in a while the mother bear woke up and licked her cubs and watched them. But she soon fell asleep again.

One day in April the mother bear awoke for good.

She sat up. She yawned.

Then, carefully, so as not to hurt her cubs, she stood on all fours and stretched her stiff, tired muscles.

The cubs were asleep. Covering them with a small branch of dry leaves, the mother grizzly left the cave.

Outside, the big bear blinked her eyes against the bright sunlight. She leaned her back against a large boulder and once again felt the sun's warmth awakening her huge, tired body.

After her long sleep with no food, the mother grizzly had lost most of her stored fat. She looked thin, but she was not yet ready to eat—now she was more thirsty than hungry.

She pushed herself to her feet and lumbered off stiffly down the mountain to a stream a short way from the cave.

Ice still covered most of the water, but the bear found a trickle in the middle of the stream and drank deeply. Then she rested under a pine tree. But soon she drank again and again of the cold mountain water.

When finally her thirst was satisfied, she ambled slowly back to her cave and cubs.

Bear Baby's eyes had opened when he was six weeks old. His ears had begun to grow, and now he was covered with soft, silky hair.

The lively little cubs were much stronger now, and they pushed their noses into every crack and corner of the den.

Early in May the mother bear took her youngsters outside the cave for the first time. Most of the snow on the mountain had melted and patches of new green grass showed. Buds had formed on the willow and aspen trees.

The old mother bear sat and looked down her mountainside to the valley below.

Her great head swayed back and forth as she sniffed the fresh spring breeze. She caught a whiff of something....

She stood and quickly started down the mountain, grunting for her cubs to follow.

Not far away, she found what she was looking for—skunk cabbage, one of the first plants of spring.

Skunk cabbage, sometimes called "bear weed," was a favorite food, and the mother grizzly ate and ate, not caring that it smelled strong and tasted bitter.

In the warm spring days that followed, most of the big bear's waking hours were spent looking for something to eat—and she ate anything she could find.

She dug for bulbs and insects.

She ate leaves and roots and grasses—and mice and squirrels, when she was quick enough to catch them.

Bear Baby was not yet four months old, and while his mother spent most of her time eating, he and his brother spent most of their time playing.

They stood on their hind legs and wrestled...their favorite game. Jumping on each other, they tumbled across the ground, rolling over and over, until they were too tired to move.

The mother bear took her cubs further and further down the mountain, but never too far from the stream.

Deer with their fawns came to drink, and once the bear family saw a huge-antlered bull elk standing knee-deep in the water.

Minks and otters swam in the trout-filled stream. And in places where it widened into a pond, muskrats and beavers built their stick-houses.

Instead of their cave, the bears now slept hidden in brushy thickets, or under the low-hanging boughs of pine and spruce trees.

The cubs were growing.

Bear Baby was bigger and stronger than his brother, but his brother was much quicker and not as clumsy.

One day the mother bear took her cubs fishing.

She waded into the stream and stood, looking at the swift, swirling waters.

She plunged her head into the stream and came up holding a silver trout in her mouth.

She carried the trout to the bank, and stripping off the sweet flesh with her sharp teeth, she gave part of the fish to her cubs.

Bear Baby liked the taste of trout.

He liked it so much that he decided to go fishing himself. He waded into the stream, but the swift-flowing waters knocked him off his feet.

"Whoof!" cried Bear Baby.

It was lucky that he was not in deep water, since he had not yet learned how to swim. Sputtering and choking, he tried to stand up, but the swirling waters pulled him down.

The mother grizzly came and carried him back to the bank.

The little bear shook himself and rubbed the water from his face and ears.

For the rest of the afternoon he sat quietly on the grassy bank on his fat haunches and watched his mother fish for their supper.

The three bears often slept during the day, but sometimes Bear Baby and his brother would wake up and play.

They romped over their mother's big, woolly body.

She grunted good-naturedly.

They nipped her ears.

She growled a warning.

They chewed on her paws—Bear Baby bit down too hard.

"GRRrrr–" growled mother grizzly, and she cuffed him on his ear.

The cub tumbled across the ground.

"GRRRRR!" Another growl sounded close.

But it was not his mother's voice.

Quickly the mother grizzly rolled to her feet. She knew that danger was near.

With a warning grunt, she sent her cubs scrambling up a tree.

A huge male bear shuffled out of the brush.

The mother grizzly rose high on her hind legs. She growled and snapped her jaws.

Male bears were very dangerous. They sometimes killed small cubs.

His brother quickly climbed to the top of the tree, but Bear Baby was in trouble.

He clawed at the bark trying to pull himself up. But he was in such a hurry that he lost his grip and began to slide downward.

He slipped close to a branch and grabbed for the limb. He wrapped his front and hind legs around the branch.

There he hung—upside down, not able to move.

"GRRRRR!" The huge male bear tramped closer.

Bear Baby clung to his limb. But the branch was not very strong.

Lower—and lower—swung the limb.

CRACK! The limb broke.

THUMP! The cub landed right on top of the big male bear.

"WHOOF!" cried the startled bear, and turning swiftly, he galloped for the woods with the cub clinging to his back.

A low-hanging branch bumped Bear Baby to the ground, but the big male bear did not stop to look back. This time the little bear was lucky—he had escaped with only a few bruises.

But from then on, Bear Baby practiced climbing a tree every day.

He learned to climb higher and higher....

Until, one day, he climbed all the way to the top of a tall pine tree.

The cubs still needed their mother's milk, but more and more they hunted food for themselves.

They dug under logs and rocks for beetles and grubs.

They tore up ant hills.

They pounced on frogs and grasshoppers.

One lucky day they found a tree with a bee hive.

The mother grizzly showed her cubs how to get the sweet-tasting honey from the bees.

She climbed up the tree to a small opening. She tore at the bark, making the opening large enough to push her paw inside. When she pulled it back out of the hole, she had a pawful of honey—and bees.

Her long hair protected her from the stings of the bees, except for on her nose. But bears love honey, and its sticky sweetness was well worth a sore nose.

She gave some honey to her cubs. They smacked their lips. From now on Bear Baby would always be on the lookout for a bee tree.

It grew hot.

The grass grew taller and sweeter.

The three bears spent the summer roaming over the mountain. Eating when they were hungry, sleeping when they were tired, and in between—playing. It was a good life.

In the mountain meadows fruit ripened on the wild
plum and the chokecherry thickets.

The bears ate all the time. One morning they came to
a gully thick with blackberries. They sat down to feast.
When finally they had eaten their fill, they stood and
waddled away. The cubs' stomachs were so full they
almost touched the ground.

Bear Baby grew taller and broader.

His thick brown hair was tipped with the silver color
that gave him his name—"grizzly." Over the summer
months he had learned many things. Now he could
swim, and fish, and climb the tallest tree. But there were
still some things that he had to learn.

One day Bear Baby wandered away from his mother
and brother. He found a gopher hole and eagerly dug at
the dirt.

   Nearby, a chipmunk sat on top of a boulder and
scolded the bear. Suddenly the chipmunk grew quiet. He
sat up...listening....

   Chittering a warning, he scampered into the branches
of a tall fir tree.

The young bear paid no attention to the chipmunk's warning. Bear Baby was so intent on his digging that he even forgot to sniff the air for scent of danger.

On the other side of the boulder a cougar lay dozing in the sun. He heard the bear's digging and lifted his head. He stretched himself to his feet, and silently, on padded paws, he moved toward the sound.

Bear Baby stopped digging. He sensed danger.

Slowly the bear walked around his side of the boulder. And slowly the cougar walked around his side of the boulder.

Suddenly the bear and the cougar met—nose to nose!

Startled, they stood looking at each other....

Then, bawling for his mother, Bear Baby turned and ran!

With a leap, the big cat bounded after him.

"GRRRRR!" Mother grizzly galloped out of the trees, growling angrily.

The cougar stopped in his tracks.

The grizzly rose high on her back legs, the hair on her arched neck standing on end.

She tore up a clump of grass and snapped her strong jaws.

The big cat backed away—he knew the signal of attack, and he knew the bear's great strength.

The powerful grizzly could break his back with one swipe of her massive paw. No animal on earth was a match for the fury of a mother grizzly.

The cougar turned and slunk back to the rocks—tonight he would hunt for a supper of ground squirrel.

The mother bear came and gently nuzzled her cub, making soft grunts of comfort.

Bear Baby moved close beside his mother. Next time he would remember to be alert.

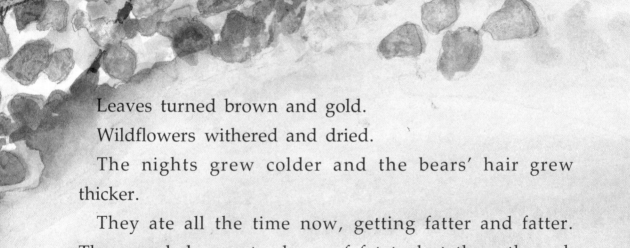

Leaves turned brown and gold.

Wildflowers withered and dried.

The nights grew colder and the bears' hair grew thicker.

They ate all the time now, getting fatter and fatter. They needed an extra layer of fat to last them through the long, cold winter ahead. Soon it would be time to start up the mountain to their den.

Late one afternoon, at the foot of the mountain, a thin curl of blue smoke rose over the treetops.

The mother grizzly smelled it first.

She sniffed the air. She knew the smell of smoke. She felt restless and uneasy, but she was not yet afraid.

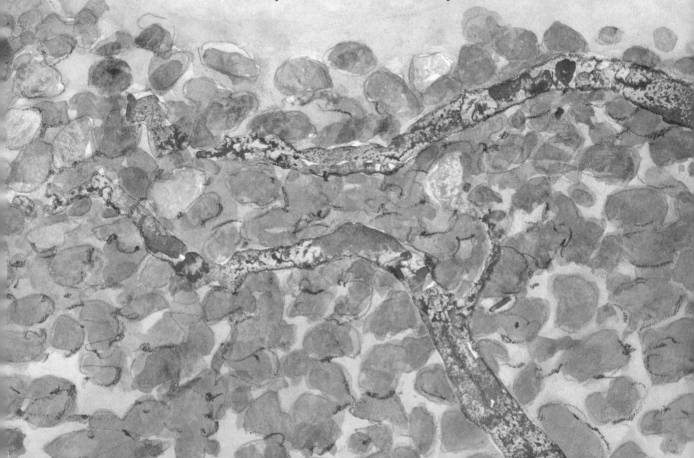

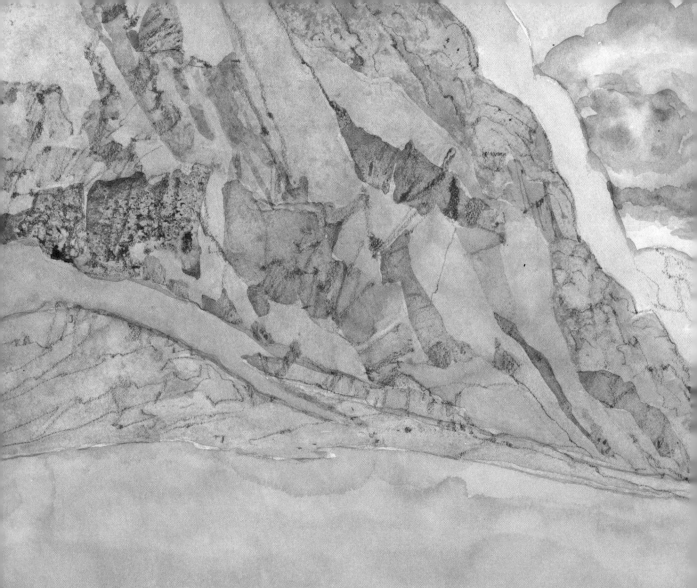

The next morning two hunters with rifles slung over their shoulders smothered their campfire with dirt. Then they began the long climb up the mountain.

Late that afternoon, a quiet breeze brought the scent of the hunters to the mother grizzly. Shaking her great head, she pointed her nose into the wind. From deep in her throat she sounded a long, low growl.

MAN! It was the only animal she feared.

The smell stirred dim memories of pain and she turned her head to lick the long scar on her shoulder where a hunter's bullet had once slashed her flesh.

Bear Baby felt his mother's fear and knew that this was a scent of great danger—something to run from, not to fight. He would remember the fearful man-scent.

Although her body was heavy and awkward, the
mother grizzly moved swiftly up the mountain, her cubs
by her side.

The time had come for Bear Baby to learn his most
important lesson of all...how to escape from man.